When a
MONSTER
is Born

For Geoffrey and Jeannette and the circle they turn—S.T.

For Rachel, James, Molly and Rosa—N.S.

Author's note:
One night, many years ago,
I was at a party in a big city in Brazil
and I heard a traditional Brazilian poem
called "When a Baby is Born . . . "
This story is based on that poem.

Illustrator's note:
Children's drawings by Emilie, Ben, Toby, and Hamish
from Great Tew Primary School

AUG 2 3 2007
Text copyright © 2006 by Sean Taylor
Illustrations copyright © 2006 by Nick Sharratt

Published by Roaring Brook Press
Roaring Brook Press is a division of Holtzbrinck Publishing Holdings Limited Partnership
143 West Street, New Milford, Connecticut 06776
First published in Great Britain in 2006 by Orchard Books, London
All rights reserved
Distributed in Canada by H. B. Fenn and Company Ltd.

Library of Congress Cataloging-in-Publication Data
Taylor, Sean, 1965—
When a monster is born / Sean Taylor ; [illustrated by] Nick Sharratt.—1st American ed.
p. cm.
"Children's drawings by Emilie, Ben, Toby and Hamish from Great Tew Primary School"—Copyright p.
Summary: Explores the options available to a monster from the time it is born, such as becoming the
scary monster under someone's bed or playing on the school basketball team.
[1. Monsters—Fiction. 2. Choice—Fiction. 3. Children's art. 4. Humorous stories.]
I. Sharratt, Nick, ill. II. Title.
PZ7.T21783Whe 2007
[E]—dc22   2006020890

ISBN-10: 1-59643-254-3
ISBN-13: 978-1-59643-254-3

Roaring Brook Press books are available for special promotions and premiums.
For details contact: Director of Special Markets, Holtzbrinck Publishers.

First American Edition June 2007
Printed in China
10 9 8 7 6 5 4 3 2 1

SEAN TAYLOR   NICK SHARRATT

When a MONSTER is Born

Roaring Brook Press
New Milford, Connecticut

When a **MONSTER** is born . . .

. . . there are two possibilities—

either it's a **FARAWAY-IN-THE-FORESTS**
monster, or . . .

. . . it's an
UNDER-YOUR-BED monster.

If it's a **FARAWAY-IN-THE-FORESTS** monster, that's that.

But if it's an **UNDER-YOUR-BED** monster, there are two possibilities—

either it **EATS YOU**, or . . .

. . . you make friends

and **TAKE IT TO SCHOOL**.

If it **EATS YOU**, that's that.

But if you **TAKE IT TO SCHOOL**, there are two possibilities—

either it **SITS QUIETLY**, does its **HOMEWORK**, and becomes the first monster to play for the **SCHOOL BASKETBALL TEAM**, or . . .

. . . it eats the **PRINCIPAL**.

If it **SITS QUIETLY**, that's that.
But if it eats the **PRINCIPAL**,
there are two possibilities—

either it growls, "**YUMMY!**"
and **DANCES BOOGIE-WOOGIE**, or

. . . it growls, "**SORRY!**"

and **WALKS OFF** through the wall.

If it **DANCES BOOGIE-WOOGIE**, that's that.

But if it **WALKS OFF**, there are two possibilities—

either it **SITS IN THE PARK** and scratches its head, or . . .

If it **SITS IN THE PARK**, that's that.
But if it sets off for the **FARAWAY-FORESTS**,
there are two possibilities—

either it finds an **EXPENSIVE HOTEL**
on the way, and decides to sleep in it, or . . . .

. . . it goes around the back of the hotel, finds a **BROKEN UMBRELLA** and decides to sleep under that.

If it sleeps in the **EXPENSIVE HOTEL**, that's that.

But if it sleeps under the **UMBRELLA**, there are two possibilities—

either a kitchen-girl comes out and tips a **SAUCEPAN OF PORRIDGE** over the monster's head, or . . .

... the kitchen-girl notices the monster

and **STOPS IN HER TRACKS**.

If the kitchen-girl tips **PORRIDGE** over the monster's head, that's that.

But if the kitchen-girl **STOPS IN HER TRACKS**, there are two possibilities—

either the monster gives her the fright of her life, "**RRROARRRR!**" and she runs off shouting, "**HELP! HELP! HELP!**" or . . .

. . . the monster gives her a rose

and they *FALL IN LOVE.*

If the girl runs off shouting
"**HELP! HELP! HELP!**" that's that.

But if they *FALL IN LOVE*,
there are two possibilities—

either she kisses the monster
and it turns into a
HANDSOME YOUNG MAN, or . . .

. . . it kisses her
and she turns into

a MONSTER

If the monster turns into a
HANDSOME YOUNG MAN, that's that.

But if the girl turns into a
MONSTER,
there are two possibilities—

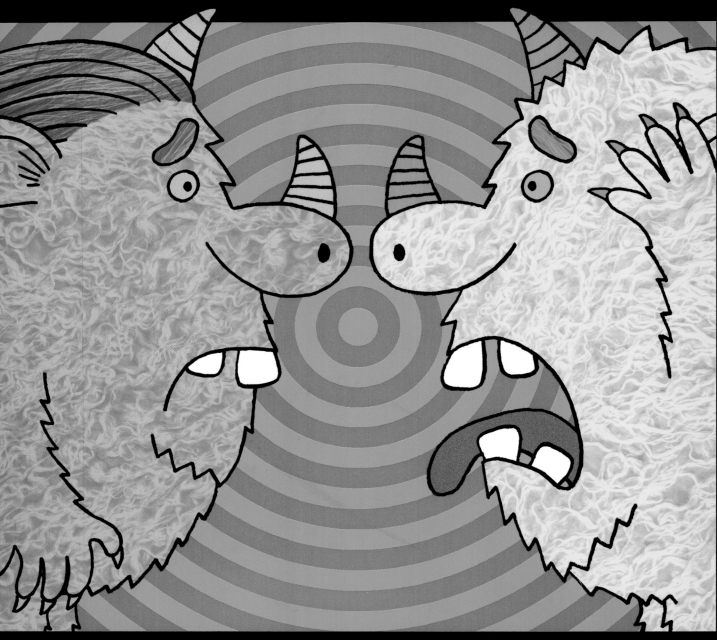

either the monster says,
"UUUUUUUUURGH!
You look horrible now!" or . . .

. . . the monster says,
"Look, I'm a monster, you're a monster.

Let's get **MARRIED**."

If the monster says,
"**UUUUUUUUURCH!**" that's that.

But if the monster says,
"Let's get **MARRIED**,"
there are two possibilities—

either the two of them live happily together
and have a **BABY MONSTER** . . .

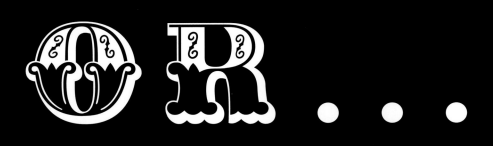

. . . they **EAT EACH OTHER**.

If they **EAT EACH OTHER**, that's that.

But if they have a **BABY MONSTER**, there are two possibilities—

either it's a **FARAWAY-IN-THE-FORESTS** monster, or . . .

. . . it's an
UNDER-YOUR-BED monster . . .